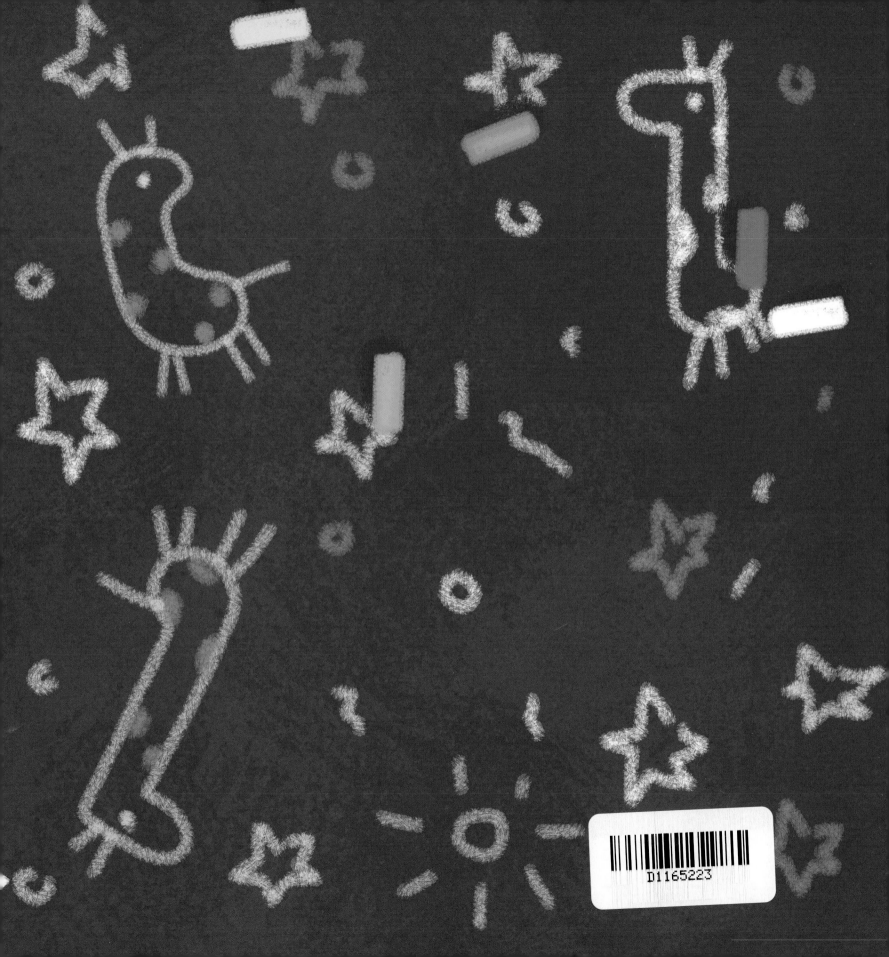

THE CHALK giraffe

written by Kirsty Paxton

illustrated by Megan Lötter

CAPSTONE EDITIONS
a capstone imprint

One day I drew
a giraffe out of chalk.
My giraffe came alive.
He could eat, he could talk!

"I'm alone!" he cried out,
"There's just gray all around."
So I drew him a tree,
growing up from the ground.

My giraffe liked that tree
with leaves blowing in the breeze.
They tickled his nose
and made him sneeze!

But still I could see
that his face looked forlorn,
peering out from among
the acacia tree thorns.

My giraffe would not laugh. Instead he just said,
"I am tired! And I can't use cement for a bed!"

So I drew him some grass. It was bright green and lush.
And soon the night came, and all was a-hush.

Till my chalk giraffe gave
a deep, grumpy sigh
and then waited for me
to make a reply.

"What's the matter?" I asked.
"It's too dark," he protested.
"I need a night-light
to get well-rested."

So I drew him a zillion
bright, white, chalky stars
and later a sun,
coming up from afar.

"Too much!" Giraffe grumbled.
"It's so bright, I can't see!
Draw me some shade
for under my tree."

"Well, I've had enough!"
I said, dropping my chalk.
"I wish I'd never drawn
a giraffe that could talk!

"Instead of saying thanks,
you make rude demands.
So goodbye, Chalk Giraffe,
you've had your last chance!"

So I rubbed that giraffe right out with my shoe.

And the stars, and the sun . . .

... and the tree that I grew.

But that night I kept thinking
of my work of art.
Sad thoughts settled
deep down in my heart.

I really missed that grumbling giraffe.
I knew I still loved him, laugh or no laugh.

The next morning
I leapt up awake.
I picked up my chalk
to fix my mistake.

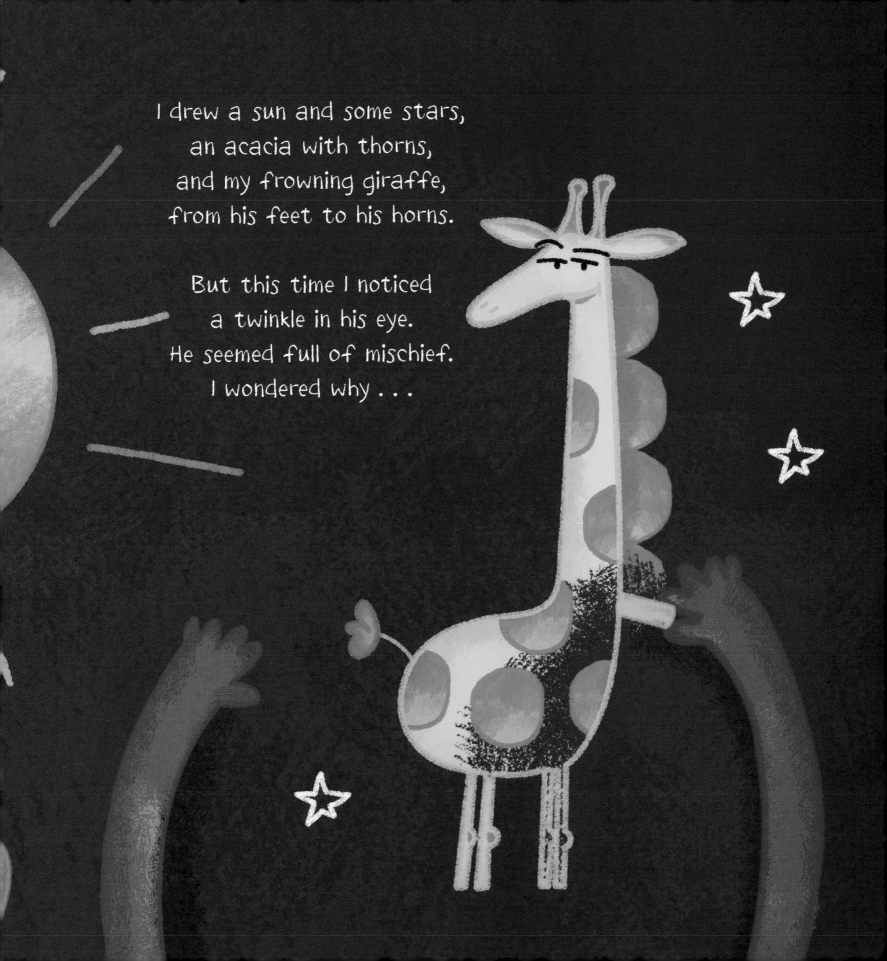

I drew a sun and some stars,
an acacia with thorns,
and my frowning giraffe,
from his feet to his horns.

But this time I noticed
a twinkle in his eye.
He seemed full of mischief.
I wondered why . . .

Then Giraffe grabbed my chalk,
and I suddenly found,
I had stick legs and arms
and was stuck to the ground!

"Come," said Giraffe,
"and look down from up here.
The world looks quite different
than it would appear."

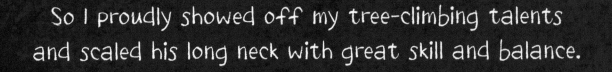

So I proudly showed off my tree-climbing talents
and scaled his long neck with great skill and balance.

And finally, perched
between his two horns,
I surveyed this new world,
and I too felt forlorn.

I saw what he saw, and it looked kind of lonely.
He needed more friends to make his home homey.

"I know what's missing!"
I cried out with glee.
"This world needs much more
than just you and me!"

So Giraffe and I got to work right that minute.
We drew zebras, a buck, and a small, spotted genet.

We drew snakes up in trees, and tiny dung beetles,
a lounging leopard, and two sprinting cheetahs.

And a rhino with horns,
and elephants with trunks,
and a croc with a grin,
looking out for his lunch.

"There's still something missing,"
Giraffe whined without end.
"Will you ever be happy?"
I asked my chalk friend.

But still I could see, from Giraffe's point of view,
there was something absent . . . a giraffe number two!

So I let my chalk friend
draw another giraffe.
It looked just like him—
except that it laughed!

I sighed with relief.
It had taken a while,
but our work was now done.
Giraffe finally smiled!

So I climbed right back down
his long, furry neck,
till I was to him
just a small, tiny speck.

When I left the chalk world,
my giraffe didn't flinch.
But I think that I saw
his right eye move an inch.

And I knew at that moment
we'd created great art,
and I was glad that I'd let
my giraffe play his part.

To Davie, Johan, and Emma,
who helped finish this story when they were
supposed to be having a bath
—K.P.

The Chalk Giraffe is published in the United States by Capstone Editions
1710 Roe Crest Drive, North Mankato, Minnesota 56003
www.capstonepub.com

Library of Congress Cataloging-in-Publication data is available on the Library of Congress website.
ISBN: 978-1-68446-096-0 Hardcover
978-1-68446-097-7 eBook PDF

Summary: A little girl's imagination springs to life when the chalk giraffe she drew on the pavement begins talking to her. But then the fickle giraffe begins making demands, and the girl must draw surroundings to fulfill his requests . . . a tree, soft grass, and animal friends. But nothing seems to please him! This delightful rhyming story escalates until they draw a laughing giraffe companion that cheers up the grumpy giraffe at last.

First Published by The Imagnary Collective (PTY) Ltd.,
t/a Imagnary House, 5 Plumer Rd, Cape Town, 7925
www.imagnaryhouse.com
Text and story copyright © 2018 by Kirsty Paxton.
Illustration and design copyright © 2018 by Megan Lötter.
All rights reserved.

Printed and bound in the United States of America.
003358

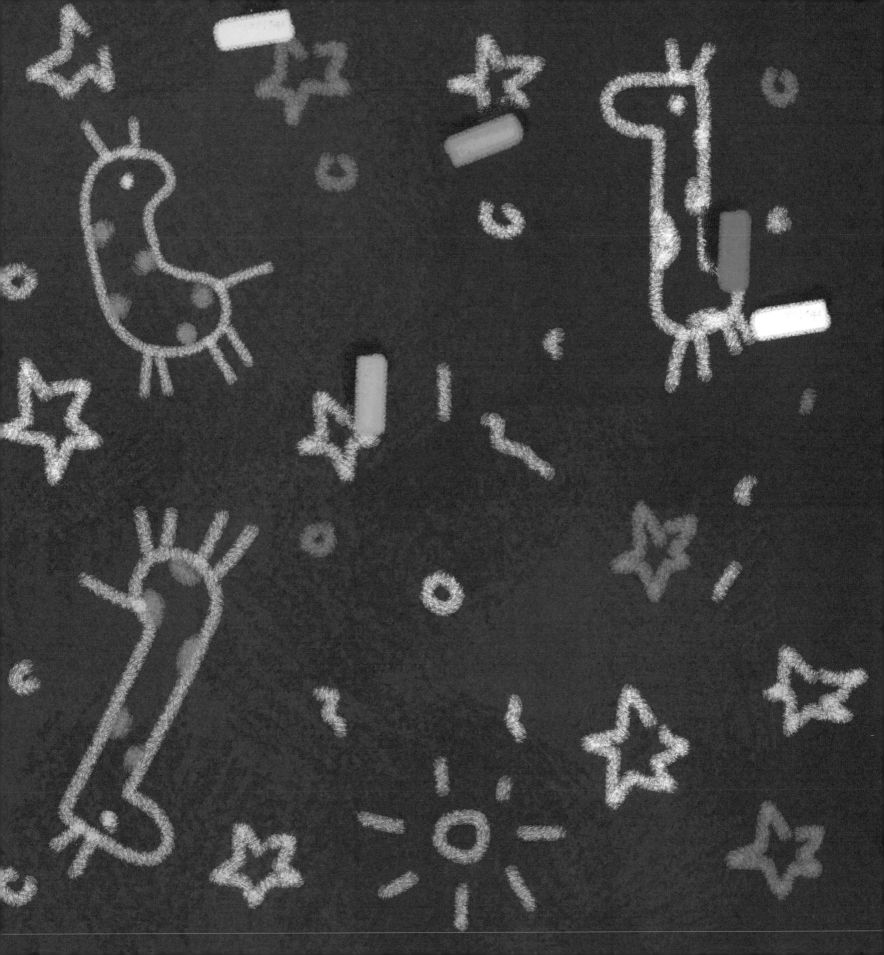